# SNOWBOY and the LAST TREE STANDING

*For Santino Ray Oram and his dad ~ H.O.*

*For my afi Guðmundur who I planted trees with ~ B.S.*

First published 2017 by Walker Books Ltd, 87 Vauxhall Walk, London SE11 5HJ · Text © 2017 Hiawyn Oram · Illustrations © 2017 Birgitta Sif · The right of Hiawyn Oram and Birgitta Sif to be identified as the author and illustrator of this work respectively has been asserted by them in accordance with the Copyright, Designs and Patents Act 1988 · This book has been typeset in Mrs Eaves · Printed in China · All rights reserved. No part of this book may be reproduced, transmitted or stored in an information retrieval system in any form or by any means, graphic, electronic or mechanical, including photocopying, taping and recording, without prior written permission from the publisher. · British Library Cataloguing in Publication Data: a catalogue record for this book is available from the British Library · ISBN 978-1-4063-5825-4 · www.walker.co.uk · 10 9 8 7 6 5 4 3 2 1

MIX
Paper from responsible sources
FSC® C101537

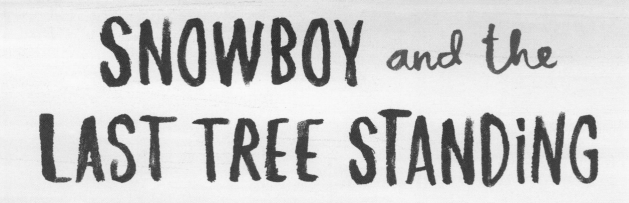

# SNOWBOY and the LAST TREE STANDING

Hiawyn Oram

*Illustrated by* **Birgitta Sif**

WALKER BOOKS
AND SUBSIDIARIES

LONDON • BOSTON • SYDNEY • AUCKLAND

# Snowboy and his Ice Troopers

were saving the Polar Bear King from the
Evil One-Eyed Emperor when Greenbackboy came up.

"I know a better game than this," he said.
"It's called KA-CHING and it starts in the forests."

"OK," said Snowboy. "I'll bring my Cloak of Many Uses."

The forests were dark. Greenbackboy's eyes lit them like moonlight.

"Right," said Greenbackboy.
"This is the game. We cut down all the trees.
  Here's your axe."

When nearly all the trees were gone,
Snowboy thought, We can't breathe without
trees, and he left one standing hidden by
his Cloak of Many Uses.

"OK," said Greenbackboy.
"All the trees have gone to make smart things.
In return for them we got this ...

## look ...

piles and piles of KA-CHING.
With it we can get anything we want.
But we want more. So on to the oceans."

The oceans were deep and ever-moving.
Greenbackboy's eyes lit them like lighthouses.
"Now," he said, "we catch all the fish. Here's your net."

When nearly all the fish were caught,
Snowboy thought,
What's a sea without fish?
A dead sea, that's what,
and he let two slip free when
Greenbackboy wasn't watching.

"OK," said Greenbackboy.
"The fish have gone to be tinned.
In return we got more KA-CHING than
anyone could ever dream of. With it we can—"
But in that moment a terrible storm
blew up, drowning his words.

As there were no trees to snag its wings, it swept all before it, tossing the mountains of tinned fish into the empty oceans where they sank and rusted and were lost.

"Back to Level Nowhere," said Snowboy. "Now what?"

"No worries," said Greenbackboy. "We're still the KA-CHING Kings. I kept it all safe in my strong box."

"Thanks," said Snowboy. "But it's no good to us now. We can't breathe KA-CHING. We can't eat KA-CHING. And I've got to get going."

He gathered his Ice Troopers and Polar Bear King
and together they trudged across the wrecked land
until they reached the last tree standing ...
saved from the storm by the Cloak of Many Uses.

Gently and lovingly they nursed
it out of its loneliness and
charmed a swarm of bees
to build a hive
in its branches.

They made a boat
and went to sea and saw
that the last two fish
had had lots of little fish
who were growing up
to have little fish
of their own.

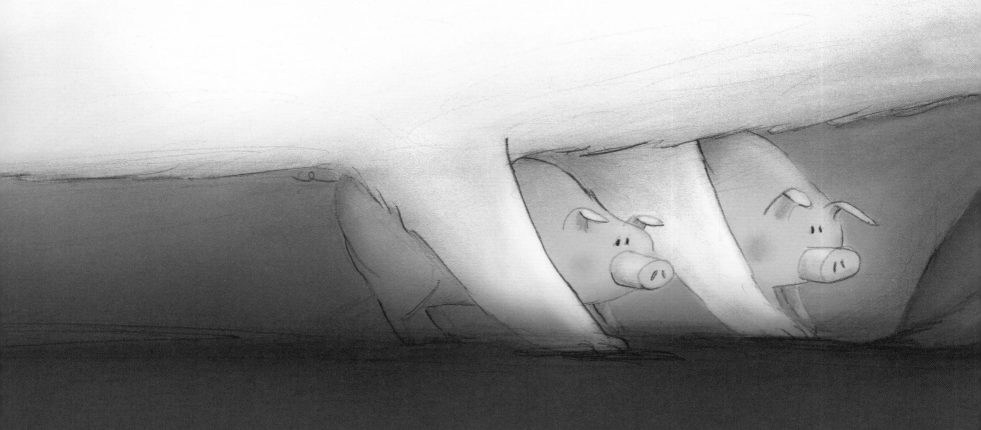

And when they got back to their tree
they found one of its seeds had taken root.
"Hurrah!" said Snowboy. "Two will become
many, many millions. Good work, Team Us!

But wait ...
who's this limping along?"

It was Greenbackboy, looking pale and as thin as a stick.
"You were right, Snowboy," he sniffed. "You can't eat KA-CHING
and I'm starving."

"Then you're in luck," said Snowboy showing him the bee hive.
"There's honey. But ask nicely and leave some for tomorrow
or be hungry again."

And with that Snowboy spread his Cloak.
As it was a Cloak of Many Uses it flew them home
where Snowboy fell happily asleep, knowing he and his team
had saved the world from the fantasy of KA-CHING ...

for now at least.